Party Time, Winnie

LAURA OWEN & KORKY PAUL

OXFORD
UNIVERSITY PRESS

Helping your child to read

Before they start

★ Read the back cover blurb together. What does your child think might happen at Winnie's parties? Do they sound like fun?

★ Look at the picture on the cover. Does it give any clues about what might happen in the stories?

During reading

★ Let your child read at their own pace, either silently or out loud.

★ If necessary, help them to work out words they don't know by saying each sound out loud and then blending the sounds to say the word, e.g. *b-r-i-ll-i-a-n-t, brilliant.*

★ Encourage your child to keep checking that the text makes sense and they understand what they are reading. Remind them to reread to check the meaning if they're not sure.

★ Give them lots of praise for good reading!

After reading

★ Look at page 48 for some fun activities.

Contents

OXFORD
UNIVERSITY PRESS

Great Clarendon Street, Oxford OX2 6DP
Oxford University Press is a department of the University of Oxford.
It furthers the University's objective of excellence in research, scholarship,
and education by publishing worldwide. Oxford is a registered trade mark
of Oxford University Press in the UK and in certain other countries

Text © Oxford University Press
Illustrations © Korky Paul

The characters in this work are the original creation of Valerie Thomas
who retains copyright in the characters.

"Winnie's Treasure Hunt" was first published in *Winnie Adds Magic* 2014
"Winnie's Giant Party" was first published as "Supersize Winnie" in *Winnie's Takes the Plunge* 2011
This edition published 2019

The moral rights of the author/illustrator have been asserted

Database right Oxford University Press (maker)

All rights reserved. No part of this publication may be reproduced,
stored in a retrieval system, or transmitted, in any form or by any means,
without the prior permission in writing of Oxford University Press,
or as expressly permitted by law, or under terms agreed with the appropriate
reprographics rights organization. Enquiries concerning reproduction
outside the scope of the above should be sent to the Rights Department,
Oxford University Press, at the address above

You must not circulate this book in any other binding or cover
and you must impose this same condition on any acquirer

British Library Cataloguing in Publication Data

Data available

ISBN: 978-0-19-276918-3

3 5 7 9 10 8 6 4 2

OX27868901

Printed in China

Paper used in the production of this book is a natural,
recyclable product made from wood grown in sustainable forests.
The manufacturing process conforms to the environmental
regulations of the country of origin.

Acknowledgements
With thanks to Catherine Baker for editorial support

Winnie's Treasure Hunt

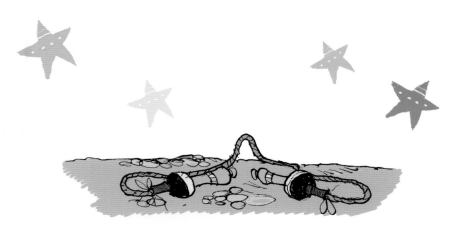

⭐ Chapter ⭐ One

It was a sunny day, and Winnie and Wilbur were skipping. Wilbur was a brilliant skipper. Winnie kept getting her legs in a muddle, so she said a rhyme to help her keep going. "One maggot, two maggots, three maggots, four. Five maggots, six maggots, seven maggots, more! I'm dropping maggots all over the floor. What the knitted noodles am I skipping for?"

Winnie paused and sighed loudly.

"I'll tell you what I'm skipping for, Wilbur. I'm as bored as a skateboard that no one skates on. Why can't something interesting happen around here?"

Just as Winnie said that, a man with an eyepatch and a wooden leg walked past. He peered closely at the ground from underneath his big black hat. Winnie thought he looked quite interesting.

"Are you a real pirate?" asked Winnie.

"Arrr!" said the man. "Good arrrfternoon, marrrm! Indeed I be a real pirate, and my name's Arrrthur."

"Are you a mean sort of a pirate who might kidnap a witch or a cat?" asked Winnie.

"Ha harrr!" said Arthur, looking fierce.

Hiss-spit! went Wilbur.

But then Arthur looked sad. "Er, no. I not be like that," he said. "Nobody likes me because they thinks I be a mean pirate. But really, I be a quiet sort of a chap who just wants to find the treasure on this map."

"Would you like Wilbur and me to help you?" said Winnie.

Arthur nodded, unrolled his map and pointed. "Yes, please, this there X marks where the treasure be!"

10

Arthur sighed. "I've looked all over those there woods, but I couldn't see an X or the treasure anywhere."

"That's because you need to fly up and look down on the whole wood," said Winnie. "Then it would look like the map."

"But you can't fly unless you be a parrot!" said Arthur.

"Yes, you witchy-well can," said Winnie, "if you hop on to my broom!"

✦ Chapter Two

Arthur hardly dared to look out of his one good eye as the broom zoomed upwards.

"There's the X!" said Winnie, pointing at two paths that crossed to make a big clear X.

"I must have been standing right on top of it!" laughed Arthur. "Let's get digging!"

Winnie flew them down and Arthur got a spade.

Then Winnie thought of something better.
She waved her wand. "**Abradacabra!**"

And instantly there was a shiny yellow
digger. She climbed into it, and soon she was
digging a hole in the middle of the wood.
Vroooom, clunk, heave!

"I can see the treasure chest!" said Arthur,
dancing with excitement. "There it is
at larrrst!"

They all dug up the chest, and then
Arthur lifted the lid. **Creak! Sparkle!**
Twinkle! Chink! There was a huge heap
of jewels and coins inside.

"Hooray!" said Winnie, putting on her
sunglasses because the treasure was so
bright. Soon, they were all trying on crowns
and necklaces and juggling with jewels.

15

"I've been trying to find this treasure all my life," said Arthur. He scratched his head. "And now I've got it, I'm not quite sure what to do with it."

Arthur bent down and tried to pick up the treasure chest. **Grunt! Heave!** It didn't move. "That be very heavy," he said. "It be a long way back to my ship from here."

"That treasure is too heavy for my broom to carry," said Winnie.

"A carrrt with wheels would do it!" said Arthur, happily. "I'd have to cover the treasure with a blanket, though. Otherwise it might be stolen."

"It would be good if it were!" said Winnie. "Then you wouldn't have to bother guarding it at all."

"Well, that be true," said Arthur. "Except if I wasn't guarding the treasure, what would I do with myself?"

"Play with your friends! Do your hobbies!" said Winnie.

"I haven't got any," said Arthur. "That's the problem!"

"I know what you could do," said Winnie. She suddenly had a very good idea.

"Have a treasure-hunt party!" said Winnie. "I'll invite my friends, and then they'll be your new friends, too."

"I've never had a parrrty before," said Arthur. "But it would be nice to have friends at larrrst!"

So Winnie got busy with her wand. **Swish!** "Abradacabra!"

⭐ Chapter ⭐ Three

Instantly the wood was decorated, and there was a table full of food. **Swish!** "**Abradacabra!**" Invitations flew off to all Winnie's friends and relations. Then Winnie and Wilbur and Arthur hid bits of treasure here, there and everywhere. "Let's make up treasure-hunt clues to help the party guests find them," said Winnie.

"Arrr?" said Arthur. "What sort of clues do you mean?"

"Wilbur, write down 'Under something that is on top of something clever'," said Winnie.

Wilbur didn't know what that meant. "Meeow?" he said, but he wrote it down exactly as Winnie said.

Wilbur and Arthur sat side by side and wrote down clues for every bit of treasure.

And then the guests arrived.

Everyone enjoyed the party very much.

After all, who wouldn't enjoy a treasure hunt

with a real pirate?

Jerry the giant found a crown that he could wear as a bracelet. Mrs Parmar looked delightful in diamonds. They all had fun, and at the end of it Arthur said, "I likes parrrties!"

He wiped away a tear. "I likes friends,
too." **Sniff!** He blew his nose on a spotted
pirate hanky. "You really be magic, Winnie.
Thanks to you, I've got friends."

"It wasn't magic that gave you friends,
you silly old pirate. It was you!" said
Winnie. "Now, stop being as soppy as
a soggy flannel! Let's get you back to
your ship."

Arthur found a cart and wheeled the rest
of the treasure along. Winnie flew overhead
to keep a lookout for thieves. When they got
back to the ship, Winnie taught Arthur a
hobby: skipping with the ropes on the deck.
Skip-bump. Skip-bump. They played until
it was time for Arthur's ship to set sail.

"Oh, gnats' kneecaps!" said Winnie when they were home. "I meant to take one sparkly-twinkly bit of treasure for myself, to remind me of a day when something interesting *did* happen. I forgot to find one!"

But when Winnie took off her hat at bedtime, she remembered that she *did* have a bit of treasure after all. "There was one clue that none of the guests got right," she said to Wilbur. "Nobody guessed that 'Under something that is on top of something clever' could possibly mean my hat!"

Winnie's Giant Party

✦ Chapter ✦
One

"It's the school fancy-dress party today!"

Winnie and Wilbur were taking a basket
of food to the school, ready for the party.
They had pickle buns, and sandwiches with
real sand and worms in them.

"We've all got to dress up," said Winnie.
"You can be Puss in Boots, Wilbur, and I'm
going to be . . ."

But Winnie wasn't looking where she was going. **Trip. Crash! Ouch!** "What's that huge log . . . er . . . leg doing there?" she said.

The sound of deep sobbing came from the bushes beside the path. **Sob! Sniff! Snob!**

"Jerry?" said Winnie. "Is that you?"

Sniff! "Yes, Winnie," said Jerry the giant who lived next door.

"What's the matter, Jerry?" said Winnie.

"It's just that there's a party . . . " he sniffed loudly.

"Yes, I know!" said Winnie. "Everyone is invited!"

"Everyone except me!" said Jerry.

"Why's that, then?" said Winnie.

"Because I'm a giant. Everybody's read giant stories in books, and now they think all giants are horrible!"

"Rubbish bins!" said Winnie. "There are some lovely stories about giants. What about that nice giant in *Jack and the Beansprout*? Hmm. Or there's the one called *The Shellfish Giant* . . . oh, I do see what you mean, Jerry!" said Winnie. "But those mean giants are just in stories — they're not real like you!"

"So why does nobody play with me?" said Jerry.

"Wilbur and I want to play with you,"
said Winnie. "Come on, let's play hide and
sneak. Go and hide, Jerry. I'll count to a
hundred, then I'll sneak up and find you."

"Goody!" said Jerry, and off he went.

Thump, thump, thump!

32

★ Chapter ★ Two

Winnie began to count. "One nitty-gnat, two nitty-gnats, three nitty-gnats . . ."

Thump, thump, thump!

"Go quietly!" shouted Winnie. "I can hear where you are! Twenty-two nitty-gnats, twenty —"

Tiptoe-crash! Tiptoe-crack!

"Ninety-eight nitty-gnats, ninety-nine nitty gnats, *one hundred*!" shouted Winnie.

"Coming, ready-steady or not!"

Winnie opened her eyes . . . and saw
Jerry's legs sticking out of a smelly-berry
bush. Just at the same moment, a little girl
saw Jerry too. **Shriek!**

"Mummy, help!" shouted the little girl, as
they both ran away.

"Er, found you, Jerry!" said Winnie.

"See, Winnie?" said Jerry. "I'm no good at
playing! And I frighten people!"

"Oh dear. You've turned hide and sneak into hide and shriek!" said Winnie. "Let's try leapfrog instead!"

Thump-bump! went Winnie. She tried to leap over Jerry, but he was too big. She just bumped into him instead. **Splat!**

"Oooh, I'm as puffed as popcorn!" said Winnie. "I give up!"

"See?" sniffed Jerry. "I told you."

"Yes, I do see," said Winnie. "But don't you worry, Jerry. You *shall* go to the party!"

"Any ideas, Wilbur?" said Winnie.
Wilbur had a think and fetched a book of
photos that showed a street party from the
olden days. "Perfect!" said Winnie.

Down on the High Street, Winnie waved
her wand. "**Abracadabra!**" Instantly there
were flowers. "I'll put these in some pots,"
said Winnie. She jumped on to her broom
and flew up on to the rooftops.

She stopped to poke flowers into all the chimney pots. "Now they're as pretty as pink cockroaches!" she said. Then Winnie flew around, scooping up washing lines from back gardens to drape them from the lampposts. "Let's use these big bloomers to make bunting!" she said.

✦ Chapter ✦
Three

Down below, Mrs Parmar was sorting out the tables and chairs and food and drink.

"Where can Jerry sit?" said Mrs Parmar. "He'd break any of these ordinary chairs!"

"Don't worry! Leave it to me, Mrs P," said Winnie. "**Abracadabra!**"

Instantly there was a giant throne of a chair. The throne sat in a hole in the ground.

"Well done, Winnie!" said Mrs Parmar.
"Jerry can use the same table as everyone
else because his chair is at just the right
height." She laid Jerry a place with a dustbin
lid for a plate and gave him a cup that was
really a bucket.

"Here they all come!" said Mrs Parmar.
"We'll have party games first, then tea. Oh,
but we should be wearing fancy dress . . ."

"Easy-peasy!" said Winnie. She waved her
wand. "**Abradacabra!**"

Winnie and Mrs Parmar were wearing fancy costumes that were as old as the book Wilbur had found. They looked lovely!

Mrs Parmar announced the first party game. "Hide and seek!"

"Dear, oh dear, Wilbur!" said Winnie. "Jerry's not very good at that. Where has he got to, anyway?"

"Meeow." Wilbur shrugged.

The children hid here and there, and just about everywhere. Some of them hid in a tree. They climbed up into its branches, then they sat and waited.

"I like it up here!" said one child.

"So do I," said another. "Did you know that Jerry the giant is coming to the party?"

The tree started to shake a little bit.

"Is he?" said a third child. "Oh, good! I like playing with Jerry."

"So do I!" said both the other children. Then there was a big splash!

"What's that? It's raining inside this tree!" said the first child.

But it wasn't rain. It was Jerry crying.

"Jerry?" said one of the children. "Are you hiding in the tree?"

"Yes, it's me," said Jerry. **Sob! Sniff!** "I'm crying because I'm so happy!"

"Jerry's costume wins the fancy dress competition!" said Mrs Parmar. "He's a wonderful tree! His prize is a book about witches."

"Oooh, just a moment, Mrs P," said Winnie when she saw the book. She waved her wand. "**Abracadabra!**"

Instantly the book changed.

"Is it a book about giants?" asked Jerry, looking worried.

"Yes, but NICE giants!" said Winnie.

"Oooh," said Jerry, and he hugged the book hard.

Jerry let the children climb all over him, and he swung them round.

Then Winnie said, "Shall we play a game
of leapfrog?"

"But . . . !" said Jerry.

"Don't worry!" said Winnie. She waved
her wand. "**Abracadabra!**"

And instantly all the children had froggy legs and froggy feet. They could leap over Jerry with no trouble at all.

Leap! Leap! Leap!

"Time for tea!" said Mrs Parmar.

They all ate their sandwiches and chatted and laughed.

Then they went down to the village pond, and the children went swimming. Their froggy legs made them swim extra fast!

And guess what? When Jerry got home he found an invitation stuck in his letter box. He'd been invited to the party all along, but just didn't know it!

"You silly great giant!" said Winnie.

After reading activities

Quick quiz

See how fast you can answer these
questions! Look back at the stories if
you can't remember.

1) In "Winnie's Treasure Hunt", how do
   Winnie and Arthur find the X that shows
   where the treasure is?
2) In "Winnie's Treasure Hunt", where
   does Winnie find a piece of treasure
   at the end?
3) In "Winnie's Giant Party", why is Jerry
   the giant unhappy?

1) they fly up on Winnie's broom and look down; 2) under her hat;
3) he thinks he hasn't been invited to the party

Talk about it!

* ★ In "Winnie's Treasure Hunt", do you
  think it was a good idea for Arthur to
  share his treasure?
* ★ In "Winnie's Giant Party", do you
  think Jerry is different from most giants
  in stories? Why, or why not?